SNAP: You Can't Keep A Secret As A Pe

Contents

Copyright 4
Introduction 5
Chapter 1 – The Swamp 6
Chapter 2 - 1 Peter 5:8 8
Chapter 3 - Thoothie 10
Chapter 4 - A Drowning In Winston 13
Chapter 5 - Missing in Winston 20
Chapter 6 - A Search in Winston 23
Chapter 7 - A Funeral in Winston 26
Chapter 8 - A Conversation 28
Chapter 9 - December 2017 30
Chapter 10 - Tina Roth 32
Chapter 11 - Jenkins Roth 34
Chapter 12 - Willy Goes Fishing 37
Chapter 13 - Mike Taylor 40
Chapter 14 - Tiffany Alexander 44
Chapter 15 – Dr. Steve Parrish 46
Chapter 16 - Night Prowler 49
Chapter 17 - The Invite 51
Chapter 18 - The Taking of Manny 57
Chapter 19 - A Masquerade Party 60
Chapter 20 - Two Weeks Later 67
Chapter 21 - A Threat Received 69
Chapter 22 - One Good Threat Deserves Another 71
Chapter 23 - A Christmas Party 73
Chapter 24 - The Lake Cottage 77
Chapter 25 - A Tragedy for Winston 80
Chapter 26 – Kyle and Bab's Lives Change Forever 83
Chapter 27 - The Ride Home 86
Chapter 28 - The Senator 88
Chapter 29 - Confronted by Conviction 91
Chapter 30 - Mike Taylor 97

Chapter 31 - Romans 12:19 99

Copyright

"SNAP: You Cannot Keep a Secret as a Pet."

This book is a work of fiction. Any references to historical events, real people, or real places are used fictitiously. Other names, characters, places, and events are products of the authors' imaginations, and any resemblance to actual events or places or persons, living or dead, is entirely coincidental.

Authors: Ace Donovan, Brock Edwards, Mickey Stone

Copyright: © 2023 by Ace Donovan, Brock Edwards, Mickey Stone

ISBN - 9798327263970

Unauthorized reproduction or distribution without the expressed written consent of Ace Donovan, Brock Edwards, or Mickey Stone is strictly prohibited.

Bible Scriptures in this book are from the King James Version.

Introduction

Helmut Schnell is a powerful man. He controls one of the largest pharmaceutical companies in the world. He has surrounded himself with senators, dignitaries from foreign countries, and fellow crooked businessmen. He keeps sheltered through crooked politicians, crooked sheriffs and even has members of the FBI on his payroll.

SNAP takes a deep dive into the world of drug trafficking, Big Pharm deceit, and even the Occult. It gives a behind-the-scenes look at what takes place in the dark and what happens when it comes into the light.

Remember… you cannot keep a secret as a pet.

Chapter 1 – The Swamp

Jimmy Jack took a long drag and blew a ring of smoke, "Dude I love this new music from AIC."

"What? Who?" Larry said.

"AIC," he said as he took another long drag and then coughed mightily.

Larry looked the way of Jimmy Jack, "Dude seriously, WTF, I don't even know what you are talking about."

Gaining control of his coughing Jimmy Jack replied, "AIC man, Alice in Chains."

Larry laughed, "AIC? Dude man, no one calls them AIC. Quit bogarting the shit and pass the Dutchie."

"Dude, look at that giant ass frog. It's huge, dude," Larry said.

Jimmy Jack squinted into the dusk, "Dude, it's like a prehistoric animal."

Larry tilted his head sideways and listened to the large bullfrog belching into the impending night.

The two boys sat and allowed the marijuana to soak through their bodies and settle in their lungs. Through the occasional giggle they talked about music, movies and of course girls' boobs, not necessarily in that order.

Larry changed the subject back to the bullfrog, "You think Kermit over there is getting a secondhand buzz," he said through a chuckle. Jimmy Jack laid back and leaned on the tree stump, "I don't know man; we should ask him. Hey Kermit, you buzzin' dude?" They both laughed and locked eyes on the frog.

Suddenly emerging from the water was a figure. A figure with large jaws. A truly prehistoric animal. It busted through the water and then opening its large jaws engulfed Kermit. Just as quickly as the creature emerged---it was gone. Gone into the shadows of the closing evening.

Larry turned to Jimmy Jack, "What the actual fuck?"

Chapter 2 - 1 Peter 5:8

> **1 Peter 5:8**
>
> Be sober, be vigilant; because your adversary the devil, as a roaring lion, walketh about, seeking whom he may devour:

Liam Hebert looked over his catch from the day. It will do, he thought. Not as good as he had done but better than some days. "Well, I suppose those bitches at Sethritch Pharmaceuticals up there in Indiana will be happy with whatever I can get 'em," he muttered out loud in his clear Cajun drawl. Looking at his catch again; about 50 baby alligator snappers, he thought.

Mike Taylor worked the receiving dock at Sethritch Pharmaceuticals. Sethritch was essential to the success of the finances and economic success of Winston, Indiana. Mike was getting closer to retirement and just was putting in his time. He seemed almost zombie-like since his wife of 24 years, Lauren, passed away after a nasty battle with breast cancer. Mike was left to raise the 20-year-old son, Wendell, by himself now. Wendell wasn't your average 20-year-old. He'd aged out of Winston Community High School. Even though Wendell was high functioning; he still had a few more needs than the average 20-year-old.

Mike continued to unload the delivery from Louisiana. As he lifted the cage, he looked around to make sure no one was watching and looked inside the package. 'Baby alligator snappers,' he thought, 'Hmmm.' He slipped one into his bucket. 'No one will miss one,' he thought. What are they doing with this many snappin' turtles at a pharmaceutical company? Mice, cats, and even chimpanzees, but snappin' turtles?

At the end of his shift, Mike hopped into his truck. He looked down into the bucket. "Well, they will do any weird stuff to one less, ain't that right, buddy," he said, as he took the turtle out of the bucket and looked into its eyes.

Chapter 3 - Thoothie

Mike Taylor made his trek to his home in the middle of Winston. It wasn't a long drive. Honestly, it wasn't a long drive anywhere in Winston. An old national gas town, it had survived because of Sethritch Pharmaceuticals. It was the biggest employer in the county. Winston was a typical smallish Mid-Western town. Winston was the type of town where everyone knew everyone, and you could expect the whole city to be at Friday night football games, Saturday night basketball games, and see each other at church on Sunday. Community was important in the bible belt and Winston fell squarely at the clasp. The barbershop and beauty shop were the best places to gossip. The grocery store was the best place to see the people that you gossip about.

If you wanted to visit a big city, you'd drive the two hours to Indianapolis or the ninety minutes to Ft. Wayne. The drive to Ft. Wayne was especially on the agenda during the winter months. The large mall featured an ice-skating rink during those months. Mike's thoughts went to last Christmas when Lauren sat at the table and laughed heartily as Mike and Wendell tried their best to master the skates. It was one of the good days that Lauren had left. There certainly weren't many of those near the end. He brushed a small tear from his eye as he arrived at home.

Wendell sat on the front porch waiting. Mike had put a swing on the front porch. He had installed it for Lauren. Lauren would sit and enjoy the birdfeeder and loved those days outdoors.

"Wendell!" Mike yelled, "Come down here, I have something for you."

"What ith it?" Wendell said in his noticeable lisp.

"Look in the bucket," Mike said.

"What ith it?" Wendell asked again.

"Wendell, look in the bucket."

"Ith a turtle. A turtle!" Wendell exclaimed.

"Not just any turtle, Wendell, it's an alligator snappin' turtle," Mike replied.

"Wow! A thnappin' turtle. An alligator thnappin' turtle," Wendell said.

"I think we need to name it Wendell. It is yours," Mike said.

"I think we should call it, Thoothie. Thoothie the thnappin' turtle," Wendell said with excitement.

"Great. Susie the snappin' turtle," Mike said.

Chapter 4 - A Drowning In Winston

Following dinner Saturday evening Wendell asked Mike if he could take Susie down to the creek to allow her some fun. "I can ride my bike. I can be home before dawk. Pweeze?" Wendell pleaded.

"Okay, okay. Look, I have to go to the store for this week's groceries and may be back after dark. I will expect to see you in the morning before church. I am planning on a big stack of flapjacks and some bacon from ol' man Smith's farm. Sounds good?"

"That sounds gweat Dad. I wuv you," Wendell said.

"Wendell you're such a good boy. I'm proud of you," Mike responded.

"Dad. I'm a man. See?" Wendell replied by showing the hair that was forming under his arms.

Mike chuckled, "You're right, Wendell. You are a man."

"You love the wadder, don't you Thoothie," said Wendell as he looked into the eyes of the turtle. Wendell sat down at the edge of the creek.

Wendell sat on a large rock and held Susie, occasionally grabbing Susie and dipping her in the water without letting her get too far away from him. Wendell heard a bit of rumbling in the tree line to his right. "You thtay here Thoothie." Wendell walked toward the tree line.

Wendell walked to the edge of the trees and looked in, trying to find the scuffling noise. What he saw "hidden" under the cover of the tree line was Kyle Roth and Barbara Stewart. Kyle was a senior at Winston High School and the star quarterback. He was generally thought of as the hero of Winston High School and the one that could bring glory to the school via a long-awaited State Championship in football. They had come close some twenty years ago led by Kyle's larger-than-life brother Mel. Mel Roth had gone on to star as a linebacker for Oklahoma and had a brief cup of coffee playing baseball for the Detroit Tigers but flamed out after a shoulder injury derailed the pitcher's career. Strangely, Mel had chosen baseball over football for fear a football career could end in injury. Mel now ran a successful timber company in upstate New York and Kyle still chased that same glory.

Barbara "Babs" was the head cheerleader and was the Homecoming Queen just last night as she celebrated the win at Winston over nearby Russell County. She had her own victory when she landed the Homecoming Queen, though it was probably a foregone conclusion. "I love you Babs", Kyle said as he gently unclasped the bra and allowed it to fall to the ground. Barbara's more than ample breasts were exposed, and Wendell was more than intrigued. She slid down to her knees, undid Kyle's pants, and began to pleasure him.

For some reason, Kyle began to look around as he moaned in pleasure. As he glanced around, he thought he saw a figure near the edge of the tree line.

"Wait, wait, wait," Kyle said.

"Why? Oh, Kyle, you were so close," Barbara muttered as she rose.

Kyle pulled up his pants struggling to get his device squeezed into his pants. The mood quickly changed as he felt for sure that there in fact was a figure there.

"Hey, Stan? Is that you? You ignorant prick!" Stan was Stan Reynolds, the star Wide Receiver for Winston and Kyle's occasional best friend. "I'm talking to you Stan, you peeping prick of a best friend," he said. Kyle walked toward the edge of the tree line.

Wendell knew it was going to be a confrontation. Wendell had been bullied by Kyle before. It wasn't unusual for Kyle to bully anyone. He had a sense of Big-Man-On-Campus. Barbara hated that about him, yet the desire to be with the BMOC outdistanced falling for someone else like Terry Ricks. Terry had had a crush on Barbara since middle school. Terry was a nice guy. A great friend and an athlete himself, but he wasn't going to be a college athlete and may not even go to college. Even though Terry was an intelligent guy, he needed to stay home and help on the farm.

"Wendell! What the hell! You freakin' retarded pervert! You are a creepy little weaselly retard. You wouldn't even know what to do with a woman like Babs," Kyle was shouting while walking slowly towards Wendell.

"I know how to kiss, and I am a man now," Wendell declared as he showed the hair under his arms.

"You are so retarded!" Kyle said as Wendell began to realize that his situation was growing more and more uncivil.

"You're wetarded. You are the wetard, Kyle," Wendell said as he turned and began to run away from Kyle.

Kyle broke into a sprint and it wasn't much of a chase. He grabbed Wendell by the back of the shirt.

"Let go of me Kyle. You are nothing but a bully. Thick him Thoothie!" Wendell screamed.

"Who the hell is Thoothie? You re-, wait, wetard," Kyle said mocking Wendell.

"Thoosie ith my thnappin' turddle," he said as tears began to form in his eyes.

Kyle began to drag Wendell as Wendell stumbled trying so hard to remain on his feet. "Where is Susie?" Kyle asked, again in a mocking manner.

"You can't have her!" Wendell screamed.

"I don't want her. I'm gonna kill her," he said to try and intimidate Wendell.

"Oh, come on Kyle, leave him alone," Barbara told him, "He's just a little pervert."

Kyle laughed and then pushed closer to the edge of the creek. He walked a few feet out into the creek carrying Wendell. "Time to swim, Wendell." Kyle tossed Wendell into the water.

"Help, I can't thwim!" Wendell began to shout as he began to panic.

"God Kyle, what have you done!" Barbara screamed.

"Oh, stop Babs. The water is like four feet deep. He just needs to stand up," Kyle responded.

"He's retarded Kyle. "Jump in, save him," she said.

"Shit, okay, but you owe me big time still," Kyle said. He jumped into the water, swam around, and then stood. "Look it's literally at my waist, he isn't going to drown, and it's cold," Kyle said.

"Are you sure?" Barbara said.

Kyle was walking back out of the water when he spotted Susie trodding along the bank. Kyle picked up the turtle, "So long Susie!" he said as he tossed Susie as far into the creek as he could.

"Sometimes, you are such an asshole," Barbara said to him.

"Oh, come on Babs. I love you," Kyle said as he slipped his hand inside of hers.

He kissed her neck and she looked at him, "Are you sure he's ok?" Barbara said. But something inside her knew.

"I'm sure. You saw how shallow the water is," Kyle replied.

They held hands, walked to Kyle's car, and got in. Kyle started the car. He slammed it in gear and spun the tires as they fled.

Chapter 5 - Missing in Winston

The alarm blared.

Mike slammed his hand on the top of the clock to stop the noise. "Ughhh," he groaned. Mike got up and shuffled to the restroom. He went about his morning routine. He got dressed for church and went about making breakfast. Flapjacks and bacon from Smitty's farm like he promised. He thought it strange that Wendell hadn't awakened from the smell and the noise from the kitchen. He was close to finishing breakfast and went to his bedroom door. He knocked, "Wendell?" He knocked again, "Wendell. Wendell, are you awake? Wendell?", he questioned as he began to knock on the door. Growing frustrated he opened the door, "Wendell, you got to get up," he said as he walked into the room. He walked over to the bed and pulled back the covers, "Wendell?" Nothing.

Wendell had a bathroom to himself. He had moved into the bedroom when his brother Jerry had gone away to the Marines. Mike was now a bit frustrated.

He rapidly walked to the bathroom door. It was already opened, "Wendell?" Again nothing. Mike now moved with a more frenetic speed as he went to the garage and looked, "Wendell?" The garage was full of 'things'. So many things that Mike no longer parked his truck in the garage. However, there was plenty of room for Wendell's bike. Wendell was a creature of habit and always parked his bike against the right side of the garage wall. Mike was stunned to find no bike.

Mike then opened the garage door and ran to his truck. He hopped in and began driving around looking for Wendell. Could he have gone for a bike ride before Mike had gotten up? Where could he be? He saw no evidence of Wendell. Was Susie there? He hadn't thought of looking in the aquarium.

The creek! It suddenly jumped into his mind. Wendell was going to the creek. He knew how to swim but would never go into the water without

Mike or Jerry. He would often argue with them; "I can't thwim!" he would say.

Mike drove to the creek and slid into the gravel. He hopped from the truck. "Wendell!" he immediately began yelling. Mike sprinted to Wendell's and his favorite spot for fishing and tooling around in the water, "Wendell!", he continued to cry out. As he approached the area, he saw Wendell's bike. "Oh God, NO!" he screamed. He ran into the water. He looked around. He dove into the water several times and went under water trying to feel for Wendell in the murkiness. Not wanting to give up, but becoming increasingly aware that he was ill-equipped to find Wendell.

He quickly exited the water. Running to his truck he began to cry and curse himself in anger. Jumping into the truck, he started the truck and swung the rear around as the back end of the truck slid and then steadied itself as he hit the road.

Chapter 6 - A Search in Winston

Mike Taylor drove as quickly as possible to the sheriff's office. He slid his truck into the parking lot coming to a stop. He jumped out not bothering to shut the door of the truck or even killing the engine. He bolted up the stairs and blasted through the door to the office.

"What the hell, Mike?" said Tuffy Moore. Tuffy rocked in his chair as he swung his feet off the desk.

"Tuffy, we got to get divers out there, we got to find him. He's missing. God Tuffy, you got to help me," Mike expressed as he began to openly sob.

Tuffy stood up quickly and said, "Who Mike? Wendell? Is Wendell missing?"

Mike merely shook his head in the affirmative. Pulling himself together, Mike was able to grunt, "I think he drowned at Foley's Creek."

"Slow down Mike. Come on, let's go find Wendell. He might be hiding or something. Let me grab my hat and let's get down to the creek," Tuffy responded, "you lead me to where you guys go on your days off. I mean, Wendell is well, you know Mike, not normal."

"I know he is slow, but he isn't stupid Tuffy," Mike said as he spun on his heels and ran back to his truck.

Tuffy followed quickly and hopped in his cruiser. Clicking on his lights, he and Mike Taylor sped through Winston and arrived within minutes. Mike turned, slammed his truck near the spot from before, and Tuffy pulled in beside him. During the short drive, Tuffy had called the sheriff and notified the folks over in St Joseph's County.

He knew they would have divers if they needed them. As much as he tried to comfort Mike, he knew.

The next two days were like a blur to Mike. The divers from St Joseph's County dove for about 90 minutes before they found the body of Wendell. Wendell had his leg tangled in some underbrush at the bottom of the creek. He undoubtedly had tried to go wading with Susie and got caught, struggled, fell, and eventually Wendell drowned.

Mike had to plan yet another funeral. He had to contact Jerry. It was miserable. The first 48 hours were miserable; the rest of his days would be spent in sadness.

Chapter 7 - A Funeral in Winston

With the outpouring of love following Wendell's death, funeral director Hubie Jones felt it would be best to have the funeral at the Winston High School gymnasium. The gym that evening was almost full to the 3100-person capacity. Mike was very moved. The city has but 10,000 and nearly half of them were there.

Pastor Waylon Jackson gave the eulogy. He, of course, spoke kindly about the 20-year-old Wendell Taylor. "No one who ever met Wendell disliked him. He was so loveable. His lisp, 'hi Pathter Jackthon' he would say." Many in attendance giggled and some laughed. One in attendance, Kyle Roth, squirmed with every minute.

"It is such a tragedy. A young man wanting to enjoy his new present, an alligator snapping turtle and just playing in the water. Drown. May God bless the Turner family. We, as a community, must reach out collectively and hug this family. We must include them in our daily prayers. Mike and Jerry need our support. The loss of a loving mother and wife and NOW the loss of a son. God bless you, Mike, and Jerry. In closing the Lord has laid this scripture on my heart, Matthew 18:6 'If anyone causes one of these little ones - those who believe in me - to stumble, it would be better for them to have a large millstone hung around their neck and to be drowned in the depths of the sea'. God bless this community, Amen," Pastor Jackson concluded.

Mike wiped the tears from his eyes. Jerry stared at his freshly polished shoes. Kyle squirmed and Barbara squeezed his hand.

Chapter 8 - A Conversation

Neither Barbara nor Kyle had any interest in viewing the body of Wendell in the casket. There were many who felt Mike Taylor should have made the decision to keep the casket closed, but Mike wanted to have those last couple of moments that he could spend. It wasn't about seeing Wendell for the last time, no, for Barbara and Kyle it was about dealing with the guilt of having left Wendell to drown that evening. On that last Amen, Barbara and Kyle were up and moving the opposite way of the casket. They were quick to the door and quick to the parking lot to Kyle's truck.

"Are we gonna talk about this?" Barbara asked.

"About what?" was the response from Kyle.

"Oh, I think you know. Kyle, you killed that little retard, Wendell," Barbara said as her voice elevated.

Kyle was clearly becoming agitated, "I didn't kiiiiilll anyone," he slurred, "We were playing. You saw; we were just horsing around. Let's be honest; you are just as guilty as me. You were there as well. You never suggested contacting help at the time."

"I know, I know, I just feel guilty. Look, your father is a powerful guy and you are THE KYLE ROTH. We can just explain it," Barbara said.

"Right, we just say, 'Hey we were at the creek smoking weed and I was dipping my stick in the oil reserve'. Just seems like easier to just let it go. We have a future together. We can get married and when I get to the NFL; we will be set for life. Shit like this always seems to come back and kill guys. I mean it's 1988.

Long-distance calls are free. Reporters have huge computers with databases. No, we aren't saying shit and we are just gonna put this away. That retard was eventually going to be a dredge on society someday anyways."

"I don't know Kyle. I know you are probably right, but it still feels very wrong," Barbara replied regretfully.

Chapter 9 - December 2017

"You bitch! I asked you to do one thing. Plan a Christmas party. It isn't hard. Call a caterer, hell, call a party planner. Helmut expects this to be a big event.

A Christmas party, with DJ," Kyle said, raising his voice and then calming back down, "I am the President of Sethritch Pharmaceuticals. You sit here all day on your ass drinking booze and doing who knows what?"

Barbara and Kyle had been together for more than 30 years now. They had been married for 26. They had two children, one a son named Jenkins. Jenkins was 24 years old and quite frankly was a disappointment to his father. He went to Purdue University with the intention of becoming an engineer. Instead, Jenkins spent the better part of three semesters chasing girls and partying to the point of basically flunking out of school and returning home. The daughter of Barbara and Kyle was named Tina, and like her parents did before her, attended

Southeast Michigan University majoring in business. Tina was far more ambitious than Jenkins, even if her intelligence paled in comparison to that of her brother.

"Oh, Imma bitch? Imma bitch? Pfff! You are such an asshole! I will get it done. I told you the call is into Reggie's. Literally the best place in South Bend. They handle everything. If that isn't good enough for you; then call someone yourself", Barbara replied as she took a long pull of her Johnnie Walker, on the rocks of course.

Barbara and Kyle were both 48 now but quite frankly they had both held their age well. Of course, it can be argued that having plenty of money allows one to make the necessary 'adjustments' you might need after 45.

"Look, I've got to go back to the office. You call Ralphie's"...

"Uhmm. Reggie's", Barbara interrupted.

"Whatever. Just call them back so we can get this done.", he said as he grabbed his jacket and headed out the door.

"Go and do that intern Tiffany! You think I don't know?!"

Chapter 10 - Tina Roth

Tina Roth laid her head on Jack Thurston's chest. "I really like you, Jack," she moaned. Jack slowly caressed Tina's nipple. "Same to you. Look, I know you are going to work for your dad. But I have big dreams. I want to be a lawyer in the city."

"Well, Winston is a city," Tina replied.

"No, I mean THE CITY as in New York. I want some Donald Trump biz, ya know. Like big money guys," Jack replied.

Tina slipped her hand between the legs of Jack and slowly stroked his manhood, "I would like to go to my parent's cottage on Lake Tippy this weekend. You know, maybe have some fun on the pontoon. Go to a secluded area, skinny dip, make love..."

"Mmmm, that sounds so good. I could use some time away," Jack said.

"You know daddy really wants a man who'll get behind me and push me to be my best," Tina said.

"Oh, I can do that," Jack said as he turned Tina over and mounted her, "I'm behind you and I will push."

They both giggled.

Chapter 11 - Jenkins Roth

"Jenkins, we are going to get a shipment tomorrow. We are supposed to get that new Coors can. I am probably going to be up at Lake Ajawameg.

Fishing should be great with this light rain we been having," Willy Swarthmore said. Willy was the 70-year-old owner and good ole boy of Willy's Lodge. Willy's was the local watering hole for Winston. "That is going to be the difference between us and that new club backed by that jackass dad of yours. What's it called? Roth's Renegades?"

"No doubt. My dad is a jackass. What is this new can about?" Jenkins asked. Jenkins was the 24-year-old son of Kyle and Barbara Roth. Jenkins was seen as a disappointment to his father Kyle. He was attending Purdue University and Kyle expected Jenkins one day to take Sethritch into the next generation. Instead, he flunked out and now worked for Willy and lived above the bar in a one-room apartment.

Willy paid him $500 a month and let him live in the apartment free of charge.

"It is this new self-cooling can. It is a can that's 'posed to hold in the cold through some new, weird technology. Imagine we won't have frosty mugs. The can stays cold, and we can save on dishes and new mugs," Willy said, "it's a win/win for me."

"That would be great. Hey Willy, I do appreciate you, you know, keeping me afloat," Jenkins said.

"Don't thank me. I'm doing more because I can't stand that pompous asshole of a dad you have," Willy said with a chuckle.

"Even better," Jenkins said as he slapped Willy on the back.

The door opened to the bar and Tina Roth stepped in. She and Jenkins have virtually no relationship except for one of animosity.

"What's up loser," Tina said.

"Oh great. Hey Tina," Jenkins replied, "what do you want?".

"I just came by to see if it was true that you are working and living in this dump," Tina replied.

"I get it. You saw the show. Now buy something or take your happy ass out of here," was Jenkins' reply.

"I'm just here to see daddy about my, uhm, paid internship this summer. Anything I need to tell dear ol' dad," Tina asked.

"Uhmmm, yep, tell him he can kiss my ass," Jenkins shouted to Tina as she walked out the door.

Chapter 12 - Willy Goes Fishing

Willy loved his private time of serenity out on the lake. He absolutely loved that private time. It allowed him to think and get clarity. It used to be a way of getting away from the Lodge so he could think about new ideas, or 'ideals' as he would say. But as he grew older it was more about just being alone and being away.

"What in the world?" Willy grunted as he dragged in the half-eaten fish. The fish, a Muskie, appeared to be half eaten and literally in half. "Who would do that, or more like what would do that?" Willy whispered to himself.

Willy went on about his fishing expedition but couldn't stop thinking about that 'thing' he'd found. He figured he would need to let Kenny Von Lucent know. Kenny was the 30-something Game Warden. Willy liked Kenny a lot more than he liked that sorry excuse for a sheriff, Lance Turner. Lance Turner never met a bribe he didn't love. Kenny, though, seemed to really love the outdoors. A guy just like those Joe Pickett novels Willy liked to read. "Reckon I will drop by the Warden's Office when I'm done," he said to himself.

Willy pulled his 1965 step-side Chevy pickup into the parking lot. Willy kept it running like a charm. The ol' three on the tree truck is a true gem and the want of many folks in Winston. Willy opened the front door and walked into Kenny's office. Much to his chagrin, Lance was sitting there chewing the fat with Kenny.

"Hey Willy! Been out there on the lake?" already knowing the answer Kenny rolled on, "What was the catch like?"

"Kenny, Sheriff," Willy said with a nod, "caught a few bluegills, enough for a meal but not enough for a fish fry," he added with a chuckle.

"Maybe you can turn it into some of those crazy good hush puppies," Kenny said.

"Hey, Kenny, look I did find something a little strange," Willy said.

"Really what's that?" the sheriff asked.

"Well, I think it makes more sense to see it than for me to talk about it," Willy added, "come on out to the truck."

"What, my truck?" Kenny said in jest.

"Just come on, ya moron," Willy said.

"What the..." Kenny asked, "You found this in the lake?"

"I did. Reckon we got some shit-bag poachers?" Willy asked.

The sheriff shook his head.

"Be the strangest poacher I ever saw," Kenny answered.

"Looks like a bear bite. But we don't have any bears here", Lance said.

"Well, it sure as hell looks more like a bite than a knife slice of a poacher", Kenny added, "I will go up there. Sheriff, want to ride along?"

The sheriff nodded yes.

"Well, alright boys. You can keep that thing," Willy added.

"Reckon I ought to," Kenny replied.

Chapter 13 - Mike Taylor

Game Warden Kenny Von Lucent pulled his State Issued Blazer into the parking lot of The Family House. The Family House was a throwback to an old general store. Owned by Glendon Morgan. Glen and his family had owned it for over 60 years. "Hey Glen, what's shakin'?" Kenny asked.

"Well, Kenny everything from the neck down," Glen replied with a chuckle.

"Hahaha, ok Glen. Came by for new traps. Had a weird find by ole Willy up at Lake Ajawameg. Need a trap big enough to trap a larger coyote," Kenny said.

Walking to the back of the store the bell rings as the front door opens again, "Hold on Kenny. I am by myself this morning. Can't seem to get help anymore. Spoiled kids just want to play video games and sit on their cell phones. Them cell phones will be the end of society," Glendon said.

Kenny just smiled and shook his head.

Well hello Mike," Glendon said.

Mike shook Glendon's hand, "Glen how ya doing? I just came by for some batteries. Got this dang battery-driven lantern and needed some for it," Mike Taylor said.

"I am in the back looking for traps for Kenny. Come on back or stay here and I can help in a moment," Glen said.

"Sure, I haven't seen the Warden in a minute," Mike said. Mike shuffled along behind Glen. Mike hadn't aged well. Only 70 years old, Mike probably looked 85. Having lost his wife and his son, Mike was just hanging on; alone.

"How ya doin, Mike", Kenny said, as he reached out his hand to shake Mike's wrinkled paw.

"I'm upright and walking, so it's a win", Mike replied.

"I would like to take you out on the new boat, Mike," Kenny said, "I found a secret spot," Kenny acted like he was whispering, "Got a place for landing big catfish."

"I would like that, Warden," Mike replied.

Glen helped Kenny find his traps and got the batteries for Mike. Mike said his goodbyes and turned to leave. At that moment, Chester Elkins, the owner of The Fish House, the best restaurant in Winston, held the door open for him. "Afternoon Mike," Chester said.

Mike nodded, "Chester."

Chester walked up to Glen and Kenny as they were finishing the traps transaction, "Wow Kenny you got Sasquatch out there somewhere?"

"Maybe," Kenny said as they all laughed.

"I don't know how Mike stays afloat. The man has looked 80 since he was 40," Chester said.

Glen nodded, "Sure has. I am not sure I could do it. Lost his wife, lost his son, and then he has that worthless Jerry. I know he is a Marine and a war hero, but why don't he take care of his dad?".

Kenny agreed, "Yep, it's a bit of a pity. But you know scripture says that the Good Lord will restore the years the locusts have eaten. Not sure how that plays out, but ya know, one day we will all know."

Chapter 14 - Tiffany Alexander

Kyle Roth stood up and slipped his jeans past his hips. He looked back at the bed where 23-year-old Tiffany Alexander lay with her ample bosom exposed. "I love you Kyle," she said as she reached up and brushed across his crotch. Kyle laid back down and kissed her hardening nipple.

"I love you too," he said, "but I got to go".

"I know you do, but I wish you would end things with Barbara so you can spend the night," she said.

"Well, I do have some news that I think you are going to love," he said with a glimmer in his eyes.

"What? Did you buy a ring?" she asked, sending back a glimmer.

"We are going to Davos," Kyle said as he stood back up and finished buttoning his jeans.

"Davos? Like Switzerland?" she said.

"Is there any other?" Kyle responded, "Not only that; you are going to meet Helmut Schnell."

"Helmut Schnell? I can't believe it! I am going to meet Helmut Schnell?" she said as she arose and pulled the sheet up past her breasts.

"That's right, THE Helmut Schnell. CEO of Sethritch Pharmaceuticals. I told you that we have big plans for you. I see you taking over the Northeast Sales Region. It should easily net you a half a mill a year. I mean, you are a hard worker and, well, you have two great assets," Kyle said with a chuckle.

"Do you mean these?" she said, sliding the sheet down and letting him have one last look before he left.

"You are making this difficult to leave," Kyle said, sitting back on the edge of the bed.

She stroked his crotch, "Well you said I can work hard things."

"Not exactly what I said, but I like where your head's at," Kyle said as Tiffany moved her head to his crotch and exposed his manhood, "Boy do I ever like where your head's at."

Chapter 15 – Dr. Steve Parrish

"Hmmmm," Dr. Steve Parrish mulled to himself. Dr. Parrish was the Aquatic Biology Professor at Northeastern Technical University in Northern Indiana. "This is very odd", he muttered. Parrish noticed a lot of dead fish. It was not unusual for him during his research to see dead fish in the river, however, this amount was more than usual. Not only the amount, but most of them were muskies. The muskie was typically the dominant fish in this ecosystem.

"So, I believe we have a new species here. What would be targeting these fish?" he said to himself out loud, "Yes, I do believe that we need to do some more research." Dr. Parrish thought through the way to maybe get a camera or some kind of way to see below the surface. Dr. Parrish felt this just simply wasn't something that was happening above the water. Dr. Parrish took several specimens and returned to campus. Meanwhile, Dr. Parrish was unaware that down river another discovery was being made.

Kenny Von Lucent went by Mike Taylor's house to get him and take him to his favorite spot for fishing.

Mike climbed into the SUV with a grunt. "Mornin' Kenny," Mike said.

"Mornin' Mike. How are you doing today? Looking forward to a big day and snatching some supper?" Kenny said.

They drove north to the Wabash River. "I got a spot that most folks don't know about. It's a little difficult to get to, but it will be worth it," Kenny said.

"I don't mind, Warden", Mike added, "I am out of the house. It seems so empty; wish the Lord would take me home."

"Ah Mike, I get ya", Kenny said.

They drove the next thirty minutes in quiet as Mike chewed his Redman Tobacco and Kenny dipped a big diesel of Copenhagen. Winter Mint to be exact. Kenny turned down a couple of country mile roads and eventually turned through a line of trees, ducked down into a gully, and eventually brought the SUV to a stop.

Kenny dropped the troller into the water and he and Mike boarded and went about a day of fishing. They spoke little and fished a bunch. They landed a dozen or so and nailed a couple of large bass. Kenny locked the boat down and hollered to Mike, "I am going to duck over here in the woods and take a leak before we leave." Kenny walked about 15 feet into the trees.

"Holy Crap!", Kenny let out a yell. Grabbing a downed limb, he slapped toward the ground.

"You alright Warden", Mike yelled out to him.

"Sure, just got the dookie scared out of me! It's a copperhead out here", Kenny yelled back to Mike.

Kenny bent down and looked at the snake, "What in the world?" he said to himself. The head was missing from the snake. He grunted and grabbed the back end that was left. He was going to take it back to the warden shack for a little more inspection.

Chapter 16 - Night Prowler

The creature crawled from the water and moved toward the farmhouse. It had left half-eaten snakes and dead fish in its wake. Crawling slowly and with a focused approach it moved toward the land owned by Mark Cramer. Mark had lived in the farmhouse for 30 years. He moved following the death of his grandfather so he could take care of his grandmother. Now 51 years old, Mark lived alone with his cherished German Shepherd. He farmed the 40 acres splitting it evenly between corn and soybeans.

Smokey started to mill around near the door. "You need out to do yo business Smokey?" The dog responded by wagging his whole back end and lifting his front paws.

"Alright, alright," Mark said as he lifted himself from his favorite rocker. The Pacers were playing terribly anyway. Mark let out the dog and decided he might get a quick smoke in on the front porch. Smokey ran around and headed towards the tall grass. "What is it, Smoke?" Mark said, taking a long drag from his Marlboro. "Probably a bunch of damn kids stealing what's left of the corn to toss at cars," he said to himself.

Smokey ran a few feet into the tall grass barking to scare off whatever intruder was lying in wait. Smokey barked louder and quicker as if he was alarmed, "yelp" was the sound from the dog. "Smokey? Smokey? Smokey! Smokey! Get back here," he called into the darkness. Grabbing a lantern he had hanging on the porch, Mark went into the tall grass looking for Smokey.

"Oh, my Lord; what in the actual hell?" Mark uttered. "Oh Smokey, what did this?" Smokey lay in two halves. Mark headed back to the house to get his cell phone.

"I think I need to give Kenny a call."

Chapter 17 - The Invite

The private jet landed at 3:30 in the afternoon, local time. Getting off the plane and walking across the tarmac, Tiffany and Kyle realized how pleasant it seemed for late October. Helmut Schnell had informed them to bring jackets or even coats if they were sensitive to the chill in the air. But today was pleasant; nearly 70 degrees. There was a limousine waiting for them; they didn't even need to go inside the airport.

"Mr. Roth, Ms. Alexander, welcome to Switzerland. I'm Charles, your driver," the tall man said as he opened the back door, "Feel free to get yourselves a drink. We should leave within ten minutes. They just need to put your luggage in the car," he added.

"Thank you, Charles," Kyle said with a nod.

Kyle and Tiffany sat in the limo. Leaning forward Kyle opened the door to the small refrigerator, "Scotch or wine?" Kyle asked Tiffany.

"Wine please," Tiffany said.

As he glanced back at her he couldn't help but take a quick look at her legs. Tiffany opened them slightly, "Do you not have panties on, Tiffany?"

She didn't answer. She simply took the drink in one hand and with the other slipped Kyle's hand under her skirt.

They arrived at Helmut's estate around 45 minutes later. "Oh my God," Tiffany whispered into Kyle's ear. This is a mansion," she added.

"Hmmm, you expected something less?" Kyle whispered back to Tiffany.

The eight-foot-tall door opened, and Charles placed the luggage in the foyer. They were met by Roger Eads, the manservant of Helmut Schnell. "Follow me."

Roger told them both, "I am Roger. If you should need anything during this week; please do not hesitate to ask me." Roger led them to a large library where Helmut sat drinking a bourbon. "Velcome Mr. Roff," he said in a German accent, "and you must be Tiffany." He rose and approached Tiffany, took her hand, and kissed the back of it. "I have heard so many vonderful tings about you."

"Oh", Tiffany said with blushing cheeks.

"Mr. Schnell, we are so thankful that you brought us over to see where the next steps for Sethritch are headed," Kyle said.

"It vill be a, uh real eye-opener," Helmut said, taking a large gulp.

They sat and made small talk for the next hour before Helmut became more direct, "Zee two of you will stay upstairs. I am sure you are exhausted. Roger will show you to your rooms. I hope you brought someting, say, sexy, maybe scandalous even," Helmut said.

"Mr. Schnell?", Kyle asked.

"Ve have a little party tomorrow with some of my friends. Very important friends," he added, "ve vill discuss in the morning," he said.

Tiffany and Kyle both slept for nearly 15 hours. The jet lag had really drained the two of them.

Roger knocked on Tiffany's door. She was still groggy but rose and slipped on a robe and stumbled to the door. Opening it slowly she asked, "Yes?"

Roger said, "Mr. Schnell shall entertain you in 45 minutes."

Roger then crossed the hall and rapped on the door of the room that Kyle occupied. Much of the scene was repeated. "Mr. Schnell eats breakfast at precisely nine a.m., Sir," Roger added to Kyle.

They arrived at the dining room and Helmut was already there. "Good morning."

They all exchanged pleasantries and had a large breakfast of fresh berries, pancakes, and sausage.

"So, you are vondering about dis evening, yes?" Helmut said, looking at his guests.

Kyle finished his orange juice, "Well yes, a bit. I am sure it is important sir."

"It is a very special engagement. I have masks for you. Many of the visitors there wish not to be recognized," Helmut said.

Kyle looked at Helmut, "Sir?"

"Vell it is, uhm how do you say, a 'lifestyle' evening," Helmut said.

Tiffany joined the conversation, "Like swingers?".

"Ve don't see it as that. It costs $10,000 for this. It isn't some seedy rundown hotel room. These are important people. Senators, businesspeople, even a Prince vill be der", Helmut added, staring at Tiffany.

"Oh, yes Sir. It's just, I've never been to such a party," Tiffany said.

"I need to know that you are our type of people, Ms. Alexander."

Tiffany replied to Helmut, "Oh I can be, Mr. Schnell. I can be."

Helmut merely nodded, "Good."

The three of them moved to Helmut's study.

"So, what is next for Sethritch? I can hardly wait," Tiffany said.

"Vell, ve are vorking on a new medication," Helmut paused, "it iz a 'cure-all'. It can extend your life and seemingly solve Alzheimer's."

"Really?" Tiffany asked.

"No, it actually doesn't. In fact, it is a highly addictive drug. Remember, Ms. Alexander, a cured patient is, well, no longer a customer. It is a placebo, but who needs to know?" Helmut said, "Are you in, Ms. Alexander?"

Kyle placed his hand on Tiffany's knee and gave a quick squeeze. "Of course, Mr. Schnell," she responded.

Helmut's gaze went to Kyle, and Kyle spoke, "I told you she would be a great, and absolutely gorgeous, I might add, addition to our growing company."

"Ve shall see," Helmut said.

Chapter 18 - The Taking of Manny

Manny Gonzalez was a ten-year-old living in Winston. He was extremely excited when he found out Winston was starting a travel soccer program: The Winston Wolves. He practiced every day, whether there was league practice or not. He walked every day to the park. Even when he was by himself, he worked on his ball handling and shooting. He was becoming increasingly good, for a ten-year-old who had never actually played in an organized league on an actual team.

Today Manny was taking the long way home. It was his idea that if he took the long way home; he could work even more on dribbling. He passed by the Hardware Store just as Billy Martz came walking out carrying his new extension cord. "Hi Manny, you are looking pretty good. A regular Landon Donavon."

"Thanks, Mr. Martz. I'm going to be even better than Landon Donavon; I'm going to be the next Messi," Manny said as he dribbled past.

As Manny turned the corner and started up Pike Street, a white van stopped, and the passenger window rolled down and Manny heard a voice. "Uh, Manny, right?"

Manny squinted and walked toward the lowered window, "I don't think I know you, do I."

"Oh, well, we have never met but I know you," the man said. "Look, I need some help. Have you seen a dog around? I can't find mine. He's just a mutt, but he is like my best friend."

"I'm on my way home. I can look," Manny replied, "what's his name?"

The man stammered, "Uh, Buster. Look, I can't really drive and look at the same time. If you could just ride. Look, we will just drive around the block. We can get ice cream for you helping."

"Ice cream?" Manny said as he picked up his ball.

"Sure. They got those new Blizzards at DQ. I promise it will be only a block," the man said.

"Okay, one block and ice cream," Manny replied as the man leaned over and helped Manny into the car.

"Better put your seatbelt on, you know safety," the man said. Manny fastened his belt and rolled down the window--- "Buster!" Manny yelled.

Chapter 19 - A Masquerade Party

Tiffany felt very sexy. She was dressed in a chiffon shirt, lacey, pink, and VERY see-through. She put on her leather pants and high heels. As she looked in the mirror, she thought to herself, 'Damn, I look good!' as she smiled. She grabbed the mask that Helmut had left for her and knew she would have a good time. Her heart raced as she thought of the potentiality of the evening.

Kyle dressed in silk pajamas. 'I am the Hugh Hefner of Winston,' he thought to himself. He chuckled as he tried to control his manhood from rising with anticipation. Kyle had gone to these parties before with Helmut, but he had never actually taken a date. Normally, he just went for the adventure of some 'strange'. He got his mask and strolled across the hall to Tiffany's room. He knocked, and Tiffany answered the door; he caught a glance of the leopard print bra through the shirt.

"Damn girl!" Kyle said.

"You like?" Tiffany said with a glimmer as she stroked Kyle through his silk pajamas, "Oh, clearly you do".

Kyle pushed Tiffany's hand aside and took a big breath, "Uh, let's not start something we can't finish now, and besides that, I took one of my, well, shall we say, testosterone pills".

They both laughed.

•••

The White Van pulled into the warehouse. "What are we doing?" Manny said as he was trying to see through his groggy eyes.

The man looked at Manny, "You will like it here. Lots of kids to play soccer with." The man lifted Manny out of the van and placed him in a makeshift cage along with about ten other younger boys. "Yep, you gonna like it here Manny."

•••

The limo arrived at a large mansion. Certainly not as large as Helmut's place, but an exceptional building, nonetheless. "Masks in place,"

Helmut said to Tiffany and Kyle. "Charles, ve vill be here until morning. You may return to the residence until then. Seven a.m. please". The door opened and the three of them went through the back door and walked to the large door. Helmut knocked. A masked man opened the door, "Invite?"

Helmut turned his arm over and showed the tattoo on his wrist.

"Welcome", the man said.

The three of them entered the main room. There were several people there in various states of clothing. There were plenty of drinks, a bowl of powder, a bowl of weed, and a bowl of what Kyle referred to as testosterone pills. Some of the debauchery had already started. A female was on her knees bent over in the "doggy" position, as she took one man from behind and was taking another in her mouth. Tiffany took a big breath. "Oh my", she whispered to Kyle, as she wasn't sure she could go on with the evening.

Helmut, sensing her skepticism, put his arm around her rib cage and gently brushed the top of her bush with the other hand, "This is where you belong, Ms. Alexander."

....

The rest of the evening was full of sinful desires. Tiffany had never been with a woman before, let alone two of them at once. She'd had some ideas of trying lesbian experimentation in college but had never followed through. But tonight, she followed through. She knew she'd had at least five men that night, and one was Helmut, and Kyle wasn't any of them.

Standing in just a thong; she was startled when a hand came from behind her and cupped her breasts gently, "Well, Ms. Alexander. Enjoying yourself?"

She recognized the voice immediately as Kyle. She turned to face him. He didn't have any clothing on and was aroused, to say the least. "This is insane. I am so tired," she said.

Kyle laughed, "You need to stay hydrated".

"Have you been to a party like this before?" she said as she gulped the beverage Kyle gave her.

"Uhmm, a couple. Quite enjoyable, I believe. I also noticed you with Marquelle and Wendy," he said.

"How do you know their names?" Tiffany inquired.

"Marquelle is Helmut's wife and Wendy is their daughter," Kyle said as he giggled.

"What!" Tiffany exclaimed as her eyes became incredibly heavy. She knew that Kyle had slipped something in that drink; at least someone had.

"Kyle?" were the last words that Tiffany ever spoke.

....

Tiffany's body lay lifeless on an altar. Six men surrounded her as they read from a large Holy Bible, a King James Version. They were reading John 3:16, only they were reading it backward. Tiffany tried hard to focus. 'What are they doing,' she thought? She could see the masks. One she recognized as Helmut and another as Kyle. She tried to move her arms and legs and couldn't. She tried desperately to sit up but seemed to lose the ability to move.

The men chanted, "All hail the Prince of Darkness." They repeated it three times. A tear began to drop from her right eye. She saw Helmut with a knife. He moved toward her, "All hail the true power of the earth," he said as he slit her wrist. Tiffany could not feel the cut, but she realized her time could be slipping. Another man held a chalice below her wrist and allowed the blood to drip into it.

"Drink this for the power and as a sacrifice to the controller of all greed, for protection, and for the power of invisibility in society. Allow us, oh Prince, to continue to control all power of the earth. Give us the guidance to know the direction for your glory. Drink", the man said as he took a swig and wiped the blood from his lips as he passed the chalice around the circle.

Helmut took the knife and slit a 6 X 6 portion of Tiffany's thigh. He stepped back as the man who had held the chalice took the slice of meat. "Oh, conquering Prince, we eat this sacrifice for the continued power and unyielding control of the flow of money in the world. We eat this as a sacrifice for your glory," the man said as he bit the flesh and passed it to the next man.

Tiffany was stunned that she felt no pain. It didn't make sense as the shock began to sit in on her mind. Helmut then took the knife, plunged it through Tiffany's chest, and twisted. Blood began to squirt from her heart. Tiffany's legs twitched and a last gasp slipped through her lips. The men cheered as they violated her lifeless flesh.

Once Helmut had finished, he turned to the man with a Goat Head mask and said, "Destroy the body".

"Yes, Priest," he said.

Chapter 20 - Two Weeks Later

There was a knock on the door. Kyle rose and went to see who would be calling on the family at 9 a.m. on a Sunday morning. He had planned on drinking and binging football all day. He had spent more time at home because there was no longer the "distraction" of Tiffany around to keep him occupied.

Kyle opened the door, "Hello dear sheriff."

"Hello Kyle. Mind if I come in and talk for a few minutes?" the sheriff asked.

"Oh, sure sheriff, anything for you," Kyle said as he pulled the door completely open and nodded toward his family room, "Drink, sheriff?"

"A little early for drinks, isn't it Kyle?"

"Juice, sheriff. Freshly squeezed orange juice" was Kyle's reply.

"Look, I don't want to take a lot of time here Kyle. Have you seen the sweet thing that interns for you? Seems she has been missing for a week or so. Her mother called me and wanted to report her missing. 'Mom' says that she calls at least once a week and they haven't heard from her," the sheriff said as he brushed the brim of his hat.

Kyle cleared his throat, "Uh, sheriff, this is a delicate situation. I took Tiffany to Davos to meet Helmut and well... Helmut took a liking to Tiffany, and she decided to stay there with Helmut. You know Helmut would want some discretion."

"I think I understand," the sheriff said. "I s'pose that I could distract the Feds about this. You know, for say, a 3-million-dollar investment."

"I bet Helmut would appreciate that gracious decision and would be more than happy to make you a rich man."

The sheriff stood and put his hat on his head. "You have a good day Kyle."

Kyle nodded and led the sheriff to the door. "Thanks, sheriff."

Chapter 21 - A Threat Received

Sheriff Lance Turner was reliving the conversation he'd had with Kyle Roth last week. He had asked for 3 million dollars. He thought he should have asked for more. He felt he could have gotten as much as five million. This missing person situation was a real shit-show. He was spending far too much time directing external investigations away from Winston and Kyle Roth. He didn't know what the truth was and it was certainly possible that the young intern was being paid handsomely to take care of any 'work' that the weird-ass Helmut Schnell would involve her in.

He rose from the table where he had shared breakfast with his wife Sandy and his daughter Sara. "Lance, you've hardly said a word. Is something bothering you?" Sandy asked. She knew the answer. He seemed preoccupied with work every day. Other than this alleged missing person, there wasn't much to worry about in Winston. "Is it that girl?"

"Sure is. I can't help but worry about what it would be like if Sara were missing. Roth tells me that she is in Sweden or something like that, but sumpin' don't feel right," he said, "I am going to the office for a bit and maybe over to the store and see what those codgers are doing." Actually, he was going to visit Roth again and see where the money was.

Turner walked onto the porch and looked at one of the large columns. There was something attached to it. "What the hell?" he muttered aloud. As he walked slowly to the column, he could feel his stomach churning.

Nailed to the column was his dog, Wendy.

"Who the hell? I'm going to kill' em". Above the head of the dead dog was a spiked letter. He grabbed it and angrily read it, "If you ever demand me to do anything again; the next bitch to die will be that sweet piece-of-ass teenager of yours, Sara. Best regards."

His stomach immediately dropped. His heart was in his throat. "Well, Mr. Schnell, we indeed shall see, you dirty son of a bitch. You are dead meat!"

Chapter 22 - One Good Threat Deserves Another

Lance Turner buried his dog and climbed inside his sheriff's cruiser. He quickly made his way to the house of Kyle Roth. Flying up the drive, dust was flying.

He rapidly hopped up the stairs and banged loudly on the door.

The door flew open, "Damn, Lance, what's gotten into you?" Kyle said as he stepped onto the large porch.

"You tell that Nazi bastard that if he ever threatens my family again, he will have much, much larger problems than some missing little floozy. I'll burn that fucking factory down with HIM in it," Lance said as he poked Kyle Roth in the chest.

"You sure that is a battle you want to have, Sheriff?" Kyle responded.

The Sheriff took a big breath and nodded, "I know he is a powerful SOB but let me tell you; my family is the only thing I care about. Don't back me into a corner."

Kyle took a step back and leaned against the closed door, "Lance, think this over. Look, come by the office first thing Monday morning and I will give you a nice gift".

"It ain't about the money now. You just relay that message," he said as he turned on his heels and quickly jumped down the stairs.

Chapter 23 - A Christmas Party

Monday morning came and Kyle Roth sat in his office and wondered if the sheriff would show up. In the top drawer of his Mahogany desk was an envelope. Inside the envelope were five $1000 dollar bills. This legal tender had not been circulated in over 50 years. He estimated each bill to be worth at least $5000. He hoped it would quiet that prick sheriff. He was reviewing resumes for a new intern when the intercom interrupted him, "Mr. Roth, the Sheriff is here."

"Sure. Send him right in," Kyle said.

The secretary opened the door and Lance Turner walked in with a serious swagger. "Kyle."

"Sheriff," Kyle said, acknowledging him.

"I might have been a little out of line there the other day, Kyle. But you gotta see it from my standpoint. He killed my dog and then threatened to kill Sara. That is some real bullshit, Kyle," Lance said, pleading.

Kyle nodded, opened the top drawer, grabbed the manilla envelope, and slid it to Lance. "Look, there are five $1000 bills in there. Also, a bundle of $100s."

Lance grabbed the envelope, "It is a far cry from three million, and where did you get a $1000 bill?"

Kyle chuckled, "Don't worry about it. Just know Helmut, uh Mr. Schnell would like this to just go away. You can expect an envelope just like that every Monday through January. It will make for a helluva Christmas for your family."

"So how much will that be in six weeks?" the Sheriff asked.

"Look, that will be about half a million. Come on Lance, you don't need three million. Honestly Lance, you know I will take care of you," Kyle added.

"Alright, Kyle, but I swear if that Nazi ever crosses my shadow; he WILL regret it," Lance added.

"Okay, Lance. Settle down," Kyle responded.

"Fuck you and Helmut," Lance said as he turned quickly and exited.

The Sethritch Christmas Party was being held at the Roth Estate. It was being held in one of the outbuildings. It would be for 550 employees and their spouses. Not all employees were invited, but it was everyone that Kyle deemed to be worthy of the party. It ended up being a great festivity and each employee there received a $1000 bonus and the employees who weren't there received a $100 gift card to Wal-Mart.

There was plenty of music and booze to be had. Late in the evening, Barbara took the golf cart back to the house for a break. Coming out of the restroom, she was alarmed to see Helmut waiting in the hall. "Hello, Barbara. You are quite lovely, and thank you for planning such a great evening."

"Thank you, Mr. Schnell," Barbara uttered.

"Uh, Helmut," he said as he took Barbara's hand and kissed it gently.

She blushed, "I was surprised to see that Tiffany isn't here with you."

Helmut allowed the statement to just pass through the atmosphere, "She chose to stay in Davos. She won't be returning to work with your husband."

"Oh?" Barbara grunted.

Helmut nodded, "Yes, her, ah, services are no longer needed by Mr. Roth."

Barbara laughed.

"You half a lovely smile, Barbara," Helmut said as he moved closer to Barbara. He placed a hand on Barbara's hip and let it slide along her curves.

"Thank you, Helmut," Barbara said as she took his hand and placed it firmly on her buttocks.

Helmut moved in closer and slowly allowed his lips to reach Barbara's.

"Oh, I don't know about this," Barbara said.

"I can assure you, it vill be okay," he said. He grabbed Barbara's hand and led her to the guest bedroom.

Chapter 24 - The Lake Cottage

Jack Thurston and Tina Roth arrive at the Roth Lake Cottage in the Spring. It was a plan for a weekend of drinking, sex, and frolic in the water. It was an unseasonal spring so far in Indiana, with temperatures staying in the 70s in the daytime and only dropping to the 50s in the evening. The first night Jack and Tina made cheeseburgers and enjoyed each other's company.

The next afternoon they decided to head out on the pontoon. It was 78 degrees in May, a true treat for Indiana. Tina was wearing a barely-there bikini. Every curve was exposed for Jack to see. They were eating some crackers and cheese on the pontoon when Tina broke the ice. "Jack, what do you see for us? You know, the future?"

Jack knew that she didn't want the truth. To him, she was a beautiful piece of ass, but she was a whiny spoiled brat. His relationship with Tina was a goal of his to get closer to her father Kyle. "Why spoil what we have now? I mean who knows? You will work for your father, and I am going to Law School, hopefully Yale".

Tina took a long drag of her beer and paused, "You may be right." She reached around and unhooked her bikini top letting her breasts soak up the sun. "You know how the water makes me horny," she said, as she stroked Jack at his waist.

"Wait. I got to take a leak. This beer is backing me up," Jack said, chuckling. "You can go ahead and get started," he laughed.
Tina slid to the edge of the pontoon and dangled her feet as she allowed her long fingers to begin to stroke below her bikini bottoms.

Jack walked to the front of the pontoon and began to urinate off the front. He had completely removed his swim trunks and was beginning to swell in anticipation.

As Tina began to pleasure herself, she felt a slight tug on her foot. As her self-massaging became more rapid, she felt another tug on her foot! This one was much harder. As she was about to climax, the next tug violently pulled Tina off the edge of the pontoon and into the water! "Shit!" she exclaimed, as she tried to sit up and see what was happening.

Then it happened. She was gone. Under the water.

"Hey you ready? I am! Look at this!" Jack yelled toward the end of the pontoon as held his manhood, "Tina? Babe?" He moved quickly to the end of the pontoon.

Jack knelt and looked over the edge. "Is that blood? Tina?" he yelled.

Jack began to panic. He jumped into the water. This was the last time either of them was seen.

Chapter 25 - A Tragedy for Winston

Sam Hagee had taken a week off work to spend some time on the water. The weather had been nothing short of spectacular for this time of year in Indiana. He absolutely loved to take his 'ship', as he called it, out for relaxation. On a lucky trip to the water, he might cop a quick glance at girls sunbathing topless. Yes sir, sometimes ole' Sam would get lucky. However, today wasn't that day.

Sam noticed the pontoon just a hundred yards or so away from him. 'That's the pontoon of the mega jerk Roth,' thought Sam. Sam had retired from Sethritch Pharmaceuticals and was happy to do so. He had spent 24 years of his life gathering trash and driving a forklift, and all he would get was an occasional gift card from Walmart.

Sometimes, though, he would catch Roth's old lady and her fake titties out for a suntan. If he was really lucky, he would see that young daughter of his and her perky boobs. He smiled to himself as he drove his boat toward the pontoon.

It seemed strange. As Sam drove closer, he couldn't see anyone moving around on the pontoon. Certainly, there weren't any boobies showing. He craned his neck to try and see anyone. "Hey Roth family," Sam called out to an empty boat. He could see the pontoon was anchored. This was certainly odd. Sam was only ten yards from the pontoon, and still no one. He began to circle the pontoon searching for swimmers. Maybe he could catch the young girl out for a skinny dip.

There simply wasn't any sign of, well, anyone. He got his boat close enough that he could toss a rope onto the pontoon and pull his boat against it. He was close enough now to board the abandoned vessel. Once aboard he saw the swim trunks of Jack Thurston and the bikini top of Tina Roth. He walked around the large pontoon. There were crackers, a cooler, and a radio playing. He turned off the radio and called out across the water, "Hello!" Nothing. Absolute silence.

The pontoon wasn't close enough for whoever was on board to swim to shore. He figured it had been about 15 minutes since he was about 100 yards from the pontoon. He grabbed his cell phone from the top pocket of his fishing shirt. "Dammit. One bar." He called 911, and after about five minutes of yelling he was finally able to get through to the dispatcher. Something was clearly wrong.

Chapter 26 – Kyle and Bab's Lives Change Forever

The Lake was heavily surrounded by sheriff's cars. Every officer and sheriff's deputy in the county converged on the area. Lance Turner was there, as was the Game Warden, Kenny Von Lucent. "What do you think happened Kenny?"

"I don't know. Maybe they were drinking, and one fell in and the other tried to save them? I doubt we ever know what really happened," Kenny said.

Kyle and Barbara Roth arrived a moment later. "Wha, what happened?" Kyle said.

"I don't know Kyle. It doesn't look good," Kenny answered, as he put an arm around Kyle Roth.

Jenkins Roth came running through the sea of cars. "Mom, Kyle, any word?" Jenkins had called his dad by his first name for three or four years. The relationship was far from father and son.

"We don't know anything. Who found the pontoon?" Kyle asked.

"Ol' Sammy Hagee. He found the empty pontoon. He doesn't know anything," Kenny said.

"That friggin' pervert. You sure he didn't have anything to do with it?" Barbara said through tears.

The Sheriff answered, "Come on, Babs. He may be a pervert, but a kidnapper? I highly doubt that."

"There's some coffee under that tent and some food. This might be a bit," Kenny told them.

Jenkins put his arm around Barbara's waist. "Come on, mom. Let's let them do their job."

"These incompetent fools?" she replied.

"Come on," Jenkins said again.

"I will be along later," Kyle said.

"Ah, Warden, would you mind if I speak to Kyle in private?" the Sheriff asked.

"Oh no, go ahead", the Warden replied and began walking towards the water.

Lance watched Kenny walk away until he was quite a few feet away from him and Kyle. "Listen, I know it may be over the line, but you think that Nazi SOB boss of yours could be behind this?" Kyle raised his eyebrows as if to ask why.

"You know, think about it. You gave me that money which clearly was in defiance of him. Maybe he did this as, well …a lesson."

Kyle stared at Lance, "He certainly isn't above this type of thing, but I just don't..." he was interrupted by two deputies running up to the two men with Kenny right behind.

"Sheriff, Kyle", Kenny said, "we found a body. Well, part of a body. It is the strangest thing I have seen. Remember those muskies?" the Sheriff nodded.

Kyle looked at the two of them, "What now? What muskies?".

Lance just took a deep breath.

Chapter 27 - The Ride Home

Barbara and Kyle started the ride home. Kyle could not contain the tears. His little girl, gone.

Barbara turned and looked at Kyle, "You son of a bitch. This is all your fault." Kyle turned and looked at Barbara as if asking why. "I will tell you why. This is karma. It's from killing that poor little retarded boy, it's for sleeping with all those young girls, the drugs, the dirty deals. This. Is. Karma," she said.

"What young girls? You are out of your ever-loving mind," Kyle said, "and besides, you were there. You didn't jump your happy ass in the water to save Wendell. That is his name, Wendell."

"Oh, you are rich. You are lecturing me about that kid? You terrorized him until you finally killed him. You know what young girls I am talking about. Only every intern that you have ever had," Barbara added, "I want a divorce. I am done with you and your lies."

"You want a divorce? You can't have one. We are in this for the long haul. maybe you forgot," Kyle said, as he raised his voice.

"Can't have one? Can't have one? We will see what Helmut has to say about that," Barbara said with a smirk.

"Helmut? Why the hell would that Nazi care?" Kyle said.

"Oh, Kyle, you moron. I have been fucking your boss since Christmas. And he is good. He is an amazing lover. Hung like a Trojan Horse."

"You BITCH! I should kill you!" Kyle yelled as he slammed his fist against the steering wheel.

They arrived at home and Barbara got out of the car. Kyle punched the accelerator, spun his tires, and left.

Chapter 28 - The Senator

Helmut was relaxing in his large chair in his office and looking across a coffee table at Senator Jorgenson. "Senator, I am sure you didn't come here to talk about zee varm veather ve are having", Helmut said.

"Well, actually Helmut. I am entertaining some dignitaries. A couple of gentlemen we both know from the Middle East. They have a, how would you say, unique taste in their preferences for company," Senator Jorgenson said as he crossed his legs.

"Go on," Helmut nodded.

"Well, I would like to purchase some 'product'," the Senator said as he drank from his glass of Scotch.

"How aged would he like his product," Helmut said.

"As I mentioned, they have unique tastes. It doesn't have to be aged for long. Anywhere from 6 to 10 years seems to be of their ilk," the Senator said.

"I see. Six to ten. I shall call Mr. McKinney. He has some aged in barrels. Would he like some snowballs to liven the party?"

"That would be a great addition", the Senator answered.

"I think I can secure four barrels and a few snowballs for say $21,000," Helmut responded.

"Thank you, Helmut. Can you secure the transported barrels to the usual location at the Hilton by Saturday evening?" the Senator asked.

"Oh please, Senator, piece of cake. With very goot icing," Helmut cracked back with a smile.

The Senator rose with a nod and handshake and left the room.

Helmut took out his phone. Not his typical cell phone, but one that most refer to as a burner. He dialed and waited.

"H. How's it hanging man?" Phil McKinley said as he leaned against his white van.

"Your lack of couth never surprises me, Mr. Mac," Helmut said. "I need to purchase some party favors. Aged in barrels for, say, 6 to 10 years."

McKinley looked at the cages where Manny sat curled up in the corner. "Uhm, I just got a new shipment. How many favors do you need and what color?"

"How about a variety? Say, two pink and two blue," Helmut said.

McKinley looked to the other cage where five girls were being held. "Indeed. I have two of each. It's gonna cost you $10,000. These are special barrels. They have yet to be opened," he said.

"Perfect Mr. Mac. The usual place, please. Saturday evening. The money will be delivered to the PO Box in Souse Bend", Helmut said and immediately killed the call.

McKinley looked to the cages and called over to his 'accomplice' Mel Goodwin. "We got a delivery this weekend Melvin."

Mel smiled exposing his gold grill, "Bet."

■■■

Chapter 29 - Confronted by Conviction

Kyle had downed nearly a fifth of Jack Daniels. He lay on the bed in his special room in the Hilton. He held a handgun and slowly put it inside his mouth. He cried. He wasn't sure if he was crying because he had the lack of courage to do what he knew he had to do. His life was spiraling out of control. His daughter was dead. Maybe it was his fault. Maybe it was karma. He was there when they killed Tiffany. He really did love her. He wanted to leave Barbara but knew the repercussions of a divorce. She would tell everyone that he was a murderer, and he was!

He knew there were children at some of the parties. My God, he thought, children. Did he really eat some of Tiffany's flesh? Did he really drink her blood? He fell asleep and dropped the gun to the floor.

The pounding on the door woke Kyle from his drunken stupor. "Go away". The pounding continued. "I said go away." The pounding didn't stop. Kyle stood and quickly fell to the floor. He couldn't quite get his drunk feet to work. He crawled to the chair by the desk and pulled himself up to walk. The pounding continued. "Stop it! I'm coming," he slurred.

Kyle opened the door and there stood Jenkins, his son, the only child he had. Kyle sobbed and sobbed hard as Jenkins held him. Jenkins carried and led his father to the bed. He laid him down and spotted the gun on the floor, "What's this Kyle?"

There was no answer as he fell back to his stupor.

Jenkins sat at the desk and found a scribbled note on the Hotel letterhead. It was clearly a poorly written suicide note. It mentioned a murder and things that were so atrocious that he could not believe what he was reading. It was disjointed but there were unspeakable things written. Jenkins sat and waited.

....

Kyle woke up. The room was spinning. He lay with his eyes shut and allowed the world to slow down. He felt his stomach churning. He got up and ran as fast as a still partially drunk man could run. He fell against the door pacing and then fell and crawled to the toilet. He lost it all.

Jenkins stood in the doorway. "Praying to the porcelain god, eh?".

"Ughhh. This is all too much," Kyle said.

Jenkins took a deep breath, "Hmmm, what part? Killing your intern? Killing Wendell Taylor? Sex with children? Helping to sell drugs under the guise of Sethritch?

Which part, Dad?" Jenkins said sarcastically. "I read your note. It certainly did not surprise me that you were not man enough to actually end it. You know you are a coward. You are a coward that you can't confess. You are a coward that you cannot kill yourself. You are a terrible person."

"Help me, son," Kyle said as he leaned against the tub.

"Help you what? And NOW I am your son? As you drop this bomb of what a terrible creature you are?" Kyle said.

Kyle drew a deep breath and then told it all. Everything. Including Helmut and his twisted life. He even talked about how Barbara was sleeping with him.

Jenkins was overwhelmed. It took a solid 90 minutes for the two of them to digest it all. This was the first time that Kyle verbalized his tangled life of sin. "I need help."

Jenkins helped his father to his feet. "You need more than help. You need to confess. You need to tell the Sheriff. Is this all true? Mom is sleeping with that walking cesspool of Devil's spit? Mom needs to know," he said, "come on."

"What?" Kyle said.

"We are going to the Sheriff," Jenkins said.

"Look Jenkins, you need to know that Sheriff Turner is crooked. He knows about Helmut," he said.

Jenkins took a big breath and then sighed, "You know what? We will ignore Turner. Let's talk to Sheriff Gunner Thompson. He is a good man. He goes to church every Sunday."

Kyle looked at Jenkins, "Going to church don't make you good. In fact, most are hypocrites. I know. Some of them are at our parties."

"Look, I know Gunner is a good man. He and I lead a men's Bible Study two days a week. Trust me; he is a good man."

....

Three hours later, Gunner Thompson, Kyle Roth, and Jenkins Roth sat in a conference room. Thompson could not believe all he had heard. "I am gonna need to contact Pat Anderson, the Prosecutor. He isn't going to believe this."

Kyle broke down again, "I need help".

"I will call Waylon, Jr.", Jenkins said. Waylon Jr. had taken over the church from Waylon quite a few years back.

"I'm going to need to lock you up, Kyle," Thompson said.

"I know Gunner. I am sorry son," he said as he turned to Jenkins.

"Let's go, Kyle. It is for your own protection. I will make sure no one knows all this. Not until we can corner Helmut Schnell," Gunner said.

"I will see you, Kyle. I need to, uh, do something," Jenkins said as he hugged his father for the first time in a decade.

Chapter 30 - Mike Taylor

Sheriff Gunner Thompson pulled into Mike Taylor's driveway. He went silently, no reason to scare Mike. How old is he now, he thought. Seventy? Seventy-five? I really don't have any idea.

He remembered that day the call came in about Wendell. He had helped dive that day. He knocked on the door.

The door slowly opened, "Hello Sheriff. Good to see you. That was some sermon that Waylon Jr. gave on Sunday, wasn't it?"

"It sure was, Mike", Sheriff replied, "I'm afraid I ain't here for chats. I'm here on business. You better sit down, Mike".

Mike turned his head to the side. "It ain't Jerry, is it? He scares me. He can be a loose cannon. He just ain't been the same since Wendell died."

"Well, see, that is why I am here Mike; not Jerry, Wendell."

"Wendell? Wendell has been gone for a long time," Mike said.

"We finally know what happened, Mike. It's Kyle Roth. He confessed to killing Wendell. It was an accident, but murder, still the same," Gunner said.

By the time Gunner had finished his sentence, Mike had melted out of his chair and fallen to the floor sobbing. Gunner bent down and helped back into the chair. They sat in silence. After twenty minutes, Gunner broke the thick air, "Can I pray for ya, Mike?".

Mike nodded.

Chapter 31 - Romans 12:19

It had been two weeks since Kyle Roth had dropped that bomb of truth. Gunner Thompson had made sure that Kyle was put in solitary. The investigation was being performed by the State Police with help from the FBI. They were checking everything that Kyle had said, including the accusations against Sheriff Lance Turner. Turner had been placed on leave.

Mike Taylor surprised Deputy Tank Elsworth when he walked into the jail. "Mike? Sheriff Thompson ain't here."

"That's okay. I have a question. Can I see Kyle Roth?" he said.

"Oh, Mike. That is probably a terrible idea. Why do you wanna talk to him?"

"Well, I want to forgive him, Tank. You can be there. I can just look through the bars," he said.

"We don't have bars anymore Mike. You watch too many movies," Tank said. "You can talk to him on that phone over there. Let me call to the back and see if Charlie can get him on the video monitor."

"Okay, whatever you need to do," Mike replied.

Tank called to the back, but Charlie didn't answer. "Who is this?"

"FBI officer Rhodes. Just watching inmate Roth. Seeing if I can glean anything," 'Rhodes' said.

"Can you get Roth on the monitor? Just be a second. I know that it isn't visitation hours, but I think this might be good for him," Tank said.

After a few minutes, Roth appeared on the screen. All that Mike could see was his face and a bit of his county-issued orange shirt.

Kyle picked up the phone, "Mr. Taylor, what..."

Mike interrupted Kyle, "Let me get this out while I can. Kyle, I forgive you. I forgive you because it is the right thing to do. Not because I like you."

Kyle began to cry. "I am so sorry, Mr. Taylor."

Mike interrupted again, "We don't need a discussion, Kyle." He hung up the phone, got up, and left.

Officer 'Rhodes' grabbed Kyle and cuffed him. "Come on inmate, back to your cell."

Kyle turned and started down the hall when he suddenly felt a sharp, cold, metal pain in his back. He dropped to his knees, "Why? What? Oh Lord, please forgive me."

The knife had plunged deep inside his back and the perpetrator lifted Kyle off the floor as he dragged the knife up his back. Rhodes was gone out the back door.

****

Helmut was floating in the water on the blowup in Barbara's huge pool. He was smiling. He spoke out loud to himself, "Wonder if Officer Rhodes has finished the business." He then broke into a large smile as a shadow cast over him. He looked up to the side of the pool. A figure had appeared virtually out of nowhere.

"Oh, it's you. Vat are you doing here?"

The figure just smiled and reached into his jacket. He pulled out a gun and aimed it at Helmut.

"Vat de hell?" screamed Helmut.

The figure pulled the trigger rapidly. He fired at least three shots into the head of Helmut Schnell as his brains exploded out the back of his head. The figure laughed and was gone as quickly as it had appeared.

Seven cars driven by different levels of law enforcement spun up the drive of the Roth Estate. Sheriff Gunner Thompson took the lead because they felt it would be less assuming, as if that were possible. Following the knock, Barbara strolled to the door and was shocked as she opened it. "Sheriff?" she said as she stretched her neck around to see the crowd of law.

"Barbara, we are here with a warrant for the arrest of Helmut Schnell. Is he here?" Gunner asked.

"Uh, well," Barbara stammered.

"Barbara, don't lie. These men here are FBI," he said. She merely stepped aside.

The lawmen spread out and moved through the house. "He is in the pool. No reason to destroy my house."

They pulled their guns and walked quickly to the sliding door leading to the pool. Gunner stepped out first. "Helmut Schnell, you are under arrest for, wait a minute.

What in the name of Moses?" he said as the lawmen saw the lifeless body of Helmut Schnell on the flotation device with his brains and gray matter floating in the water of the pool

.

∙∙∙

Mark Cramer stood on his porch as he watched his new pug puppy, named Betsy, play in the yard. He was thinking about how God had blessed him with all this land. He was glad that he could allow people like Jerry Taylor to hunt on his land. Betsy frolicked into the high grass.

Mark gave a quick whistle and called, "Betsy. Get out of there. I really need to get an electric fence." He bounced off the porch as he heard Betsy begin to bark uncontrollably. A moment later he heard the unmistakable sound of a shotgun blast. Betsy came bounding out of the high grass as quickly as possible.

Mark picked her up and took her into the house. She continued to stand at the door and bark as Mark walked into the high grass. Mark pulled out his .22 pistol. It was a family heirloom passed down from his great-grandfather. As he walked into the high grass, maybe five feet into the area, he almost slipped on a wet grisly substance. "What in the world?" It was then he saw a turtle with its head blown completely off at the shell.

He looked around and saw nothing.

■···■

After a long day hunting and seeing that ridiculous snapper turtle, the man got into his Blazer and fired it up. He rested his right arm on the steering wheel and rolled up his sleeves. There, on his right forearm, was a tattoo: 'RIP Wendell'.

****

Dr. Steve Parrish continued his study of the lake. He was casting a large net and then pulling it in. Not sure what he was looking for he continued casting and catching cans and boots. As he pulled it in a last time before calling it quits, he was amazed. He looked at the egg. "Is that a snapping turtle egg? It can't be…"

Made in the USA
Columbia, SC
14 October 2024